Blusie
The Little Blue Bird

Gladys Sanchez

outskirts
press

For my amazing and loving nieces and nephews Evan, Kevin, Juliana, Soli, Ava, Anelie, and Alyssandra, who encouraged me to publish a simple bedtime story I told them during a Christmas sleepover.

This Book Belongs to:

_____

CHAPTER 1
Fly Like A Torpedo

Blusie, the little blue bird, was only three weeks old when she found her home on a beautiful oak tree overlooking Beverly Glen Boulevard almost a year ago. From this tree, Blusie had a commanding view of the cars that whizzed by pretty much every hour of the day. Protected behind the oak tree stood a gray-colored, stucco home that belonged to a family of four: a young girl, not much older than six years old, her ten year old brother, and their parents. Blusie did not know their names. All she knew was that she wanted so badly to be a part of that family. Not a day went by that she did not voice her wish.

"One of these days," Blusie said again one autumn afternoon, "I am going to fly right into that house and find my place among that family."

"Be careful what you wish for, Blusie," responded her neighbor bird. "You may not like it in there."

"Oh, but I will," insisted Blusie. She flew right down to the windowpane and looked inside. She could see the high, beamed ceiling over the living room. "There!" she pointed out. "I'll perch my nest right in that corner on that wooden beam."

Just then, the little girl came out of her bedroom and crossed into the kitchen. Her brother followed. They were dressed for school, but still looked very sleepy. Their mother and father, dressed for work, walked into the room. They sat together at the breakfast table and started eating. Blusie admired them for a while, then she flew back to her branch on the oak tree. "I'll be the happiest bird in the world."

"If you insist, Blusie," said her neighbor bird, unconvinced. "Now you just have to figure out a way to get inside." And that there was the rub. How to get inside? Blusie sat quietly, thinking, while her neighbor bird sang. She thought and thought and thought, but nothing came to mind.

Then, the front door opened. Blusie perked up. The neighbor bird stopped singing. The little girl came out, carrying her schoolbag over her shoulder. Her brother followed her out, holding his books under his arm. Finally, the parents came out, putting on their jackets and pulling out their keys.

"You kids have a good day at school," the father said before he kissed his wife good-bye.

"See you tonight," they responded. Then they were off.

"That's it!" exclaimed Blusie. "When they come home, they have to open the door to walk inside."

"Naturally," the neighbor bird replied. "Same as they did last night and the night before and the night before, and so on, and so on, and so on."

"Well, that will be my chance. As soon as they open the door, I'll take off from this tree and I'll fly in as fast as a torpedo before they close it again!" The neighbor bird thought about it.

"It may work."

"It's gonna work! Just you wait and see."

Blusie spent the entire day sitting on her branch, waiting for the family to come home. She did not want to risk missing her chance to fly inside the house behind them. In the meantime, her neighbor bird flew errands, dug for worms, and enjoyed flying from neighborhood to neighborhood visiting with friends.

At last, Blusie saw the mother's car pull into the driveway, followed by her husband's. Blusie perked up on her branch and exercised her wings in preparation to make her entrance. Her neighbor bird returned just in time.

"Here's my chance!" exclaimed Blusie.

"Blusie, maybe you should think twice about what you're doing," the neighbor bird warned. But Blusie ignored her. The little girl, her brother and their parents walked up to the front door. The father unlocked it, and threw it open for his family to pass through. Blusie took off towards the opened door like a torpedo in water. It was the fastest she had ever flown in her entire life. The door was so wide open, Blusie was certain nothing could keep her from making it inside. But just as she got to the doorway and was about to cross the threshold, the father slammed the door shut. Blusie crashed right into the glass and dropped to the ground. Her beak was bent out of joint, and her feathers were rudely ruffled. But what hurt Blusie the most was that her dream of finding her place inside the house, among the family she so much admired, was dashed.

Heartbroken, Blusie sat on the ground watching the family inside go about their business. Her tears just kept rolling down her cheeks. Her neighbor bird said not a word, for she knew there was nothing she could say to make Blusie feel better. She just watched her quietly. Finally, Blusie flew back onto her branch. She was emotionally drained and exhausted. She yawned.

"Get some sleep, Blusie," the neighbor bird advised. "Tomorrow is another day." Just as Blusie was about to close her eyes, the front door opened. The mother stepped out, carrying a scarecrow on a bamboo stick. She dug the scarecrow into the ground and next to it a wooden sign that read: Happy Halloween.

Blusie's eyes grew wide with excitement. "That's right!" she yelled. "It'll be Halloween in a week!"

"So it will. What of it?" asked the neighbor bird.

"There will be hundreds of children coming around the house asking for candy. Which means that they'll be opening the door countless of times, and they'll be leaving it wide open and long enough to pass out candy. I'll have all the chances I need to find my way inside!" With that thought, Blusie went to sleep with new found hope.

CHAPTER 2
Happy Halloween, Blusie

It was finally Halloween and Blusie was excited. Gone from her mind was the memory of her failed attempt to enter the gray-stucco house a week earlier. Her complete focus was on Halloween and the opportunity it now presented. She flew above the neighborhood, looking for the first sight of children walking around in their costumes.

"It's still too early," said her neighbor bird, who flew beside her. "It's only two o'clock and the children are still in school."

"Halloween should be a national holiday," insisted Blusie. "It's not fair to make children go to school and make them wait six, long, dreadful hours before going trick-or-treating," she continued. "Why, how can any teacher expect them to sit in class and pay attention when the only thing on their minds has to be the candy they'll be collecting tonight?"

"Nevertheless, they are in school, and it's only two o'clock." Just then, Blusie and her neighbor bird heard a distant thunder. Blusie surveyed the sky and saw rain clouds forming in the distance.

"Oh no!" cried Blusie. "Rain will cancel Halloween!" Without any warning, a gust of wind kicked up, practically stopping Blusie and her neighbor bird in mid-flight. The wind blew too strong for their wings to propel them forward.

"We better get back to our tree," shouted the neighbor bird over the howling wind, "before we break a wing!" Blusie and her neighbor bird hurried home. They got back just in time to take shelter from the rain that began pouring down.

"It's not fair!" Blusie pouted. "It's simply not fair!"

"The gray sky is crying, the blue bird is trying, to come to grips with the drip, drip, drip that's ruining all her chances," the neighbor bird sang. Blusie sat on her branch, disappointed to say the least.

It must have rained four hours straight. The streets were flooded. Cars driving by splashed mud and water all over the place. This Halloween was not turning out the way Blusie had hoped. She sat on her branch with the longest frown ever seen on any bird.

"Happy Halloween, Blusie," her neighbor bird said, offering her a worm for a treat, in the hopes of cheering her up." But it did no good. The sky turned dark and the clouds moved over the moon, covering it up and diminishing any light it radiated.

It must have been an hour later when Blusie heard the family's cars pull into the driveway. She saw the little girl, her brother and parents hurrying to get inside.

"But, Mommy, why can't we go trick-or-treating? Why can't we?" the little girl cried, wearing her princess costume. "I don't mind the rain!"

"The storm has knocked out all the power across town," her father answered.

"We're not afraid of the dark!" countered the brother, wearing his pirate costume.

"It's not safe, dear," replied their mother. With that, they made their way inside and the door shut behind them. The house remained in darkness but for a single candle the little girl's mother lit and placed on the dining room table.

"There's no hope now," Blusie lamented.

"Maybe all's not lost, Blusie. There's a saying that goes 'In the darkest hour of night, look for the cloud with the silver lining, for that will get you through the plight.'"

Blusie looked up at the sky. It was filled with clouds of all shapes. She looked hard for the one with the silver lining, but couldn't find it. Suddenly, the cloud veiling the moon started to break apart. Moon rays streaked out in thin lines, illuminating the gray-stucco house. Then the rain stopped. The city lights below sparkled once again, like little jewels on a dark blanket. All power returned. Blusie turned around and saw that the home she yearned to enter was lit once again.

"Trick-or-treat, trick-or-treat, give me something good to eat," a group of children sang as they came around the house in their Halloween costumes, holding their pumpkin buckets. One of the children rang the doorbell.

"Oh boy!" Blusie exclaimed. "There is hope again!" She flapped her wings, preparing to launch for the door. The neighbor bird watched the little girl open the door. She was still in her costume, but this time, she was holding a large bowl full of candies and started passing them out. "It's Halloween time!"

"Happy Halloween, Blusie," her neighbor bird said somewhat sadly.

"Here I go!" Blusie took off with the widest smile on her beak. But as she arrived at the doorway, she suddenly stopped and screamed! "AHHHHH!" She had never seen anything so frightening in her life before. Hanging from the ceiling inside were ghosts and skeletons with bloody, red eyes, and green witches flying on their brooms, and spider webs all over the furniture. On the beam, where she dreamed of nesting for the rest of her life, crawled a large, black spider with large fangs. "I'm scared!" Blusie screamed and quickly turned away and flew back to her branch. She was trembling so hard that the branch shook under her feet.

The neighbor bird laughed so hard she almost lost her balance. "Silly, Blusie," she said. "They're only decorations."

"I don't like them. They'll cause me to have nightmares. I can never have a good night sleep in there so long as those dreadful, creepy, scary things are hanging inside."

"Well, you had a chance. Too bad you weren't brave enough to seize it." Blusie slumped her shoulders. She watched for hours as kids came and went, came and went, came and went, until they stopped coming — until Halloween came to an end.

The neighbor bird could hear Blusie sniffle back her tears. "Cheer up, Blusie. It will be Thanksgiving in a few weeks. Maybe they'll let you in then. People are always much friendlier on Thanksgiving Day."

"That's right!" Blusie remembered. "It's the day that all friends are welcomed into everybody's homes! I'll certainly be let in, won't I?"

The neighbor bird knew there was only one answer Blusie wanted, and it pained her somewhat to give it, but at last she did. "On Thanksgiving Day, Blusie, all friends will be welcomed." Blusie's hopes returned.

"Then I'll wait for Thanksgiving Day!" With that last thought, Blusie said goodnight and fell asleep. The neighbor bird let out a quiet sigh then closed her eyes.

CHAPTER 3
A Thanksgiving Greeting

Three weeks came and went and Thanksgiving finally arrived. Blusie woke up that morning feeling very optimistic that she would finally be invited to join the nice family she had been admiring for more than a year.

"I suppose today is the day," her neighbor bird said, with a hint of skepticism.

"Today is," agreed Blusie. Just then, the little girl, her brother and their mother walked out of the house.

"All right, kids," the mother said as they hurried to the car, "we're on a mission to find the biggest, fattest bird to serve at our dinner tonight." They jumped into the car and drove off.

"Did you hear that?" a concerned Blusie asked. "They'll be inviting for dinner only the biggest, fattest bird they find." Blusie saw three large, fat crows on a telephone wire above the house. Then a strong, brown hawk made his presence known by gliding not too far over the ridge. "I don't stand a chance!"

"Blusie, I think you got it all wrong."

"Quick, help me chase them off!" said Blusie, as she flew off to confront the crows. But the neighbor bird just shook her head and remained on her branch.

"Shoo, crows, shoo!" ordered Blusie. The crows looked at one another, quizzically, wondering about Blusie. "You can't stay here. It's my house!"

"Ah, little blue bird, fly away and leave us be. We're not bothering anybody," replied one of the three crows.

"But you are. Me! You're here to take my place inside that house and I'm not going to let you!"

"We're here for no such thing, blue bird," said the second crow. "We're on our way up to the top of that tall mountain on the horizon. We're just taking a short rest before we fly on."

"I don't believe you!"

"Well, it's the truth. Besides, we're free-flying birds. The last thing we want is to be caged up in a box," explained the third crow.

"Now, fly back home, kid," advised the first crow. "I'm sure if your mother knew you were out here quarreling with the likes of us, she wouldn't like it."

"I don't have a mother. I never met her," said Blusie with a hint of sadness. The crows just looked at each other and said no more. Just then, the hawk above the ridge let out a loud screech. Blusie turned her attention towards him and flew to confront him.

"Hello, there," greeted the hawk. "What brings a little bird like you over my ridge?"

"I'm not little. I'm big and fat."

11

"Relatively speaking, I'm sure. What can I do for you?"

"It's Thanksgiving Day," said Blusie.

"So it is. It's the day to give thanks for what we have. And I am grateful for this ridge I call my home. It provides for everything I need. You're more than welcome to visit whenever you please, blue bird, for we're friends now that I have made your acquaintance. Happy Thanksgiving." And with that, the hawk continued to search for its Thanksgiving prey.

Blusie flew back to her tree where the neighbor bird waited for her. "They won't leave," she reported. She paced her branch, thinking of a plan. "I got an idea!" She flew into the garden and started digging for worms. She ate and ate and ate.

"Blusie, I think you got it all wrong."

"I gotta eat so I can get big and fat," Blusie responded. She ate and ate and ate some more, until her belly grew like a balloon and she toppled over. "I feel nauseous," Blusie moaned. Then, she let out the loudest, most thunderous belch ever, which scared the crows, and the hawk, and all the other birds in the trees away. The neighbor bird laughed.

"Well, Blusie, you did it. You chased away the big birds. I should remember never to underestimate you again." Blusie flew happily back to her branch. She saw the little girl's mother pull into the driveway.

"Here I go. Wish me luck!" Blusie flew around the doorway in the hopes that the little girl's mother would spot her and invite her inside. But all her wishing was in vain. The mother, the little girl and her brother did not even notice Blusie. They just walked inside the house with all their grocery bags.

"Did you find a big bird?" Blusie could hear the father ask.

13

"Sure did," replied the mother.

"The biggest and fattest one there was!" added the little girl right before she shut the door. Blusie's face grew long with sadness. For a long moment, silence lingered. Finally, the neighbor bird spoke up.

"We can have our own Thanksgiving dinner out here, Blusie," she said in the hopes of cheering Blusie up. "Sure, I'll fix up something really good. I'll just go find some sunflower seeds and worms…"

"Oh, must you mention worms?" interrupted Blusie, holding her belly. She flew away to be alone for a while.

It was four hours before Blusie made her way back to her branch. The sky was dark, and the Thanksgiving celebration inside the house was under way.

"Happy Thanksgiving, Blusie," the neighbor bird said.

"What's so happy about it?" a crestfallen Blusie asked. "I'm not the bird being served inside."

"You should be so thankful, Blusie."

Blusie and the neighbor bird saw the family and their friends taking their seats at the dinner table. It was crowded with all the trimmings that customarily accompany the main meal, including corn on the cob, stuffing, spinach casserole, cornbread, mashed potatoes and pumpkin pie. "Everything looks delicious," commented Blusie. "But where is the bird? He hasn't arrived and they're going to start dinner without him."

"Oh, he's coming," warned the neighbor bird. Just then, the mother pulled out a large turkey from the oven. It was golden brown. "And there he is." Blusie's beak dropped open in disbelief as she saw the little girl's mother place the turkey in the middle of the table. The father grabbed a sharp knife and large fork and started carving it.

"What's happening!" exclaimed Blusie.

"Silly, Blusie," the neighbor bird laughed. "I told you that you had it all wrong. The traditional Thanksgiving dinner is a big, fat turkey. You were never in consideration."

"You mean, it was never in their thoughts to invite me inside for dinner?" Blusie's neighbor bird shook her head. Blusie flew down to get a better look at the Thanksgiving festivity. She envied all the friends that had been invited into the little girl's home. "What's it going to take?" Blusie asked under her breath, pressing her beak up against the glass. Just then, the little girl looked over her shoulder and spotted Blusie staring inside. She was mesmerized by her beautiful, blue feathers. She stood from the table and walked over to the window. Blusie

could hardly believe that the little girl had finally noticed her. Blusie smiled. The little girl smiled back and waved. Blusie fluttered her right wing in response.

"Come back to the table, sweetie," the mother said. The little girl obeyed. Blusie looked up at her neighbor bird, thrilled that contact had finally been made.

"Maybe all you need now is a Christmas wish," said the neighbor bird.

"Yes, Christmas! The happiest day of the year." Blusie flew up to her branch.

"Now, you just have to wait five weeks for Santa Claus to come."

"I'll wait," Blusie assured her neighbor bird. "I'll wait gladly." Blusie fell asleep, thinking about Christmas.

CHAPTER 4
Santa Claus Comes To Town

Christmas Eve arrived quickly and nobody was happier about it than Blusie. "He's coming tonight!" she exclaimed. "Santa Claus comes to town tonight!" She flew around for hours, observing the beautiful Christmas decorations. She saw families and friends visiting with each other, carrying Christmas gifts to exchange. Blusie could hear Christmas music spilling out from many homes. It was a sight to behold.

When the sun went down and the moon started to come out, Blusie made her way back to her oak tree. She saw the Christmas tree all lit and all the Poinsettias decorating every corner of the little girl's house. Then, she heard Christmas Carolers approaching, singing "Silent Night." The little girl, her brother and parents came out to listen.

"I've never heard anything so beautiful in all my life," Blusie declared. She joined in the singing by whistling along. That drew the little girl's attention.

"I've never heard anything so beautiful in all my life," the little girl said, referring to Blusie's singing. The Carolers continued on to the next house, and the little girl and her family went back inside. Just then, the neighbor bird arrived, carrying in her beak a package wrapped in Christmas paper.

"I got you a Christmas present, Blusie" her neighbor bird announced. She gave Blusie the little package. "It's not much, but I do hope you like it."

"Oh, it's beautiful," said Blusie, touched by her neighbor bird's kind gesture. She quickly unwrapped the package and found a beautiful "BFF" necklace. She quickly put it on. "I love it very much. I will never take it off for as long as I live," she promised. Then, she remembered that she did not have a present to give to her friend. Blusie hung her head low. "I'm afraid that in all my excitement getting ready for Santa Claus to come, I forgot to get you a gift."

"Oh, that's okay, Blusie," her neighbor bird said. "You have already gifted me your unconditional friendship." Blusie threw her wings around her neighbor bird and embraced her tightly.

Inside the house, the little girl, dressed in her night gown, walked over to her

bedroom window. From there, she could see Blusie embracing her neighbor bird. She closed her eyes and started to pray. Her parents walked into the room. "Come on, little one," said her mother, "it's time for bed. Santa Claus will be coming soon, and you need to be asleep."

"Okay, mommy." The little girl jumped into bed, all excited. "I hope Santa Claus brings me everything I wished for."

"I'm sure he will," the little girl's father assured her. They kissed each other goodnight. Within minutes, all the lights in the house, except those on the Christmas tree, went off.

Blusie surveyed the neighborhood. "It won't be long now," said her neighbor bird. They waited patiently together.

The night was very quiet and still for hours. It was the most peaceful night Blusie had ever known it to be. Then, in the distance, the faint sound of jingle bells could be heard. Blusie and her neighbor bird perked up. They knew Santa Claus was approaching. The jingles were getting louder and louder, and then a red light appeared in the sky. It got bigger and bigger as it got closer and closer. Then, Blusie and the neighbor bird saw Santa Claus on his sleigh being pulled by nine reindeer.

"He's here," whispered Blusie with quiet excitement.

"Blusie, are you sure living inside that house is what you want?" asked the neighbor bird. But before Blusie could answer, Santa Claus made his presence known.

"Ho, Ho, Ho!" Santa Claus shouted. He navigated his sleigh onto the little girl's rooftop. The nine reindeers landed gently and brought the sleigh to a complete halt. Blusie and her neighbor bird saw Santa Claus grab his large, toy bag and climb down from his sleigh. He made his way to the brick chimney. Blusie flapped her wings, preparing to launch. The neighbor bird knew there was no chance to change Blusie's mind. Down the chimney went Santa Claus with his toy bag. Blusie took off and followed him down the chimney. It worked! Blusie was finally inside the little girl's house.

"Good-bye, Blusie," said the neighbor bird under her breath. She had never known sadness like she did that night.

Santa Claus landed inside the house with a quiet thump. Blusie flew right over him and made her way onto the beam in the corner where she always dreamt her home would be. From there, she had a clear view of Santa Claus while he worked to place the toys the kids had asked for under the tree. One by one, Santa Claus placed eight presents under the tree, among them a two wheel bike, a dollhouse, a football, a doll stroller and a several board games. There was one more gift left in the bag. He hesitated to pull it out. Blusie watched quizzically. Then she saw that Santa Claus had spotted her. She grew nervous.

"Hello there, Blusie," Santa Claus said.

"You know my name?"

"Oh, yes," responded Santa Claus. "I know every little girl's and boy's name and everything they wished for all year long. But I also listen to the wishes made by the little creatures living in this world. Yours especially."

"Then, you know what I've been wishing for?"

"Yes," Santa Claus nodded. "It's why I let you follow me inside." Santa Claus walked closer to Blusie. "But before I can let you stay, I need to know for sure, Blusie, if this is indeed truly what you want."

"Oh, yes, Santa Claus! It is truly. I've dreamt it for so long to be a part of this family. I've never had a family of my own. I want to belong to this one. There is so much love here. I know I'll be happy. I just know I will."

Santa Claus was immediately convinced. "All right, then, Blusie. I will happily deliver your Christmas wish, as well as little Molly's." Blusie looked at all the presents under the Christmas tree. She saw that half of them were for the little girl named Molly. Blusie's heart was instantly filled with love.

"She wished for me?" asked Blusie.

"From the moment she saw you Thanksgiving night, she hasn't stopped wishing for you." Santa Claus pulled out a white bird cage from his bag and opened the little door. "In you go, Blusie." Blusie happily flew into the cage, which Santa then placed under the tree. He hung a label with Molly's name on it. "Merry Christmas, Blusie."

"Merry Christmas, Santa Claus." Santa Claus grabbed his bag and made his way back up the chimney. Blusie could hear him climb onto his sleigh again. She heard the reindeer hoofs galloping on the roof, and then they were gone.

"Ho Ho Ho, Merry Christmas!" Blusie heard Santa Claus shout. Then, silence again. She closed her eyes with the happiest smile on her beak. Her dream had come true on Christmas night.

Outside, the neighbor bird watched Blusie for a moment. Then, she closed her eyes.

Christmas morning was exactly how Blusie had imagined it would be. The little girl and her brother ran into the living room and went straight for the tree. The first thing the little girl saw was the pretty, white bird cage. Inside of it, she found Blusie. "Oh, Mommy and Daddy," exclaimed the little girl, "it's exactly what I wanted! Her name is Blusie!" The little girl's parents smiled at the joy Blusie brought her. "I know just the place to put her." While her brother began opening his Christmas presents, the little girl took the cage and ran into her room. She placed the cage on the night table next to the big, bay window. "Perfect!" She ran out of the room and left Blusie alone.

Blusie flew around the cage happily. She was finally part of the little girl's family. "Perfect!" she echoed.

CHAPTER 5
Happy New Year, Blusie!

For five days, Blusie was the happiest bird in the world. She loved her pretty, white bird cage, the view from the nightstand, and spending time with the little girl. But she started feeling a little weak in the wings, and she didn't understand why, until her neighbor bird flew across her window for the first time since Blusie flew into the house. Blusie realized that it had been almost a week since she last spread her wings and flew. Blusie suddenly had the urge to fly, but she couldn't. She was locked in her cage.

"Where is Molly?" she asked herself. "And why hasn't she taken me out flying?" She started feeling lonely. She looked around, waiting for the little girl to come see about her. Hours went by and the little girl still did not come.

Blusie struggled to spread her wings. They started feeling heavier and heavier with every passing hour. Blusie grew more and more concerned. "What's happening to me?" Again, she saw her neighbor bird fly across the window, no doubt heading back to her branch on the oak tree. Blusie longed to go to her. She realized she missed her greatly. Blusie hopped around her cage, trying to catch her neighbor bird's attention, but it was no use. Blusie's sadness started to overwhelm her.

It wasn't until eight o'clock in the evening that the little girl and her family returned to the house. The little girl ran into her room and straight to her cage. "Hello there, Blusie! I hope you had a great day. I missed you. But I'm home now."

Blusie started hopping around the cage, twiddling. If the little girl understood twiddling, she would have heard, "Please, Molly, take me outside! I want to spread my wings! I want to fly again! Please, take me outside for a little while!"

But instead, the little girl understood that Blusie was hungry. "Oh, are you hungry, Blusie? No problem, I'll fix it right now." The little girl sprinkled a few bird seeds into the cage. "There you are. Enjoy your dinner, Blusie. And goodnight! I'll see you in the morning. It's New Year's Eve tomorrow and we're going to a party." The little girl threw a white sheet over the cage. She changed into her nightgown and jumped into bed. Then, she turned off the lights. The room went completely dark.

"I'll be alone all day again tomorrow," Blusie told herself. She remembered the words her neighbor bird said a few months earlier: "Be careful what you wish for, Blusie. You may not like it in there." Blusie cried herself to sleep.

The next morning, the little girl lifted the white sheet from the cage and found Blusie slumped on her wooden swing. "Good morning, little bird! Oh, how I love you! Here is your morning breakfast, and a little water to hold you over the whole day." But Blusie was too weak to thank her. "I'll be gone the entire day, but I'll be back after midnight to wish you Happy New Year! It'll be a new year after midnight! New Year, new beginnings! That's what my daddy says. Well, good-bye, Blusie." The little girl ran out of her room.

Blusie looked out the window and saw all the birds flying freely in the sky. But she didn't see her neighbor bird. "Where are you?" she asked. "Why haven't you come to see about me? You were right. As much as I love Molly and her family, this was never meant to be my home." Blusie tried to hop around, but she felt very weak and tired, and she fell to the bottom of the cage. She tried getting up, but couldn't. "But I loved it while I lived here. I finally had a family."

The little girl and her family came home at twelve thirty the next morning. The little girl's parents quietly entered the room and laid their daughter in bed. They kissed her goodnight and left the room again.

As soon as the sun entered the room, and she felt the sunrays kiss her face, the little girl jumped out of bed. As she ran to the cage, she yelled out "Happy New Year, Blusie!" But her joy soon gave way to concern when she found Blusie at the bottom of the cage. "What's the matter, Blusie?" she asked. But Blusie did not reply. "Wake up, Blusie!" But Blusie did not move. "Blusie! Blusie!" The little girl's parents and brother heard the little girl's screams and ran into the room. "Blusie won't wake up!" cried the little girl. They saw the little blue bird lying on the cage floor. The little girl ran into her mother's arms.

"Come, little one. I'll explain what happened." Her mother took the little girl into the living room while the little girl's dad and brother cleaned out the cage.

"Where should I put her?" asked the little girl's brother.

"Put her in the garden," replied the father. "I better go see about your sister. I know it's breaking her heart." The brother took Blusie into his hands and walked outside. He laid the little blue bird in the garden next to the pretty, orange flowers that adorned it, then ran back inside.

The neighbor bird's heart broke when she saw Blusie lying in the garden. She saw the BFF necklace she gave Blusie for Christmas still hung around her neck. It glistened under the sun. The neighbor bird flew to her and laid a gentle kiss on her forehead. "Come back home, Blusie."

The little girl, still crying, ran out of her house and darted towards the garden. Startled, the neighbor bird flew back to her branch. "I know what will make her strong again," the little girl said. She cupped Blusie in her hands and looked up at the oak tree. She found Blusie's nest. She climbed up the tree. When she reached Blusie's branch, she gently laid Blusie back in her home. "You'll be safe here, my little Blusie. I love you." The little girl climbed down again. But instead of going back inside, she watched for a long moment.

The neighbor bird looked over at Blusie. "Wake up, Blusie," she said. "You're home again!" A gentle wind blew and made the branches dance gracefully. A few seconds later, Blusie slowly opened her eyes. She took a deep breath, which made her wings strong again. She stood up, much to the neighbor bird's delight. "Welcome back, Blusie."

"I'm home again?" asked Blusie.

"You are," assured the neighbor bird. "Somebody who loves you very much was strong enough to let you go." Blusie looked down at the little girl, who was now crying joyful tears at the sight of Blusie feeling well again.

Blusie flew down to the little girl and flew around her many times. The little girl jumped up with happiness. "Happy New Year, Blusie! I love you," the little girl said.

"Happy New Year, Molly! I love you," Blusie twiddled. She flew up towards the sky and the neighbor bird joined her. And indeed, it was a very happy new year for Blusie and her friends.

The End.

CPSIA information can be obtained
at www.ICGtesting.com
Printed in the USA
BVHW062012040122
625448BV00019B/836